Why not?

Also by Bel Mooney

I don't want to!
I can't find it!
It's not fair!
But you promised!
I know!
I'm scared!
I wish!
Why me?
I'm bored!

for older readers

Joining the Rainbow
The Stove Haunting
The Voices of Silence

Bel Mooney

Why not?

Illustrated by Margaret Chamberlain

mammoth

First published in Great Britain 1990
by Methuen Children's Books Ltd
Published 1992 by Mammoth
an imprint of Egmont Children's Books Limited
Michelin House, 81 Fulham Road, London SW3 6RB

Reprinted 1992 (three times), 1993, 1994 (three times),
1995 (twice), 1996 (three times), 1997 (twice), 1998 (twice)

Text copyright © 1990 Bel Mooney
Illustrations copyright © 1990 Margaret Chamberlain

The right of Bel Mooney and Margaret Chamberlain to be
identified as author and illustrator
of this work has been asserted by them in accordance
with the Copyright, Designs and Patents Act 1988.

ISBN 0 7497 0860 3

A CIP catalogue record for this title
is available from the British Library

Printed and bound in Great Britain
by Cox & Wyman Ltd, Reading, Berkshire

Contents

Explain!

Kitty always used to say she didn't want to do this or that. Then there was a change – *she* wanted to do things, but the grown-ups wouldn't let her. Instead of saying, 'I don't want to!' she found herself asking, 'Why not?' Very often.

One day, for example, she asked Mum if she could walk to school on her own. 'No,' said Mum firmly.

'Why not?'

'You know why not,' smiled Mum.

'No I don't!'

Mum thought. 'Well, because you might have an accident.'

'But there's a lollipop lady!'

'Anyway, you're too young.'

'Lots of my friends go to school on their own. So why not me?'

'*Because.*' Mum wasn't smiling now.

'Because what?' asked Kitty.

'Because I said so,' said Mum, folding her arms.

'That's not a good reason,' said Kitty.

When she went to school she told William and Rosie what had happened. 'Oh, my mum always says that,' sighed Rosie.

'So does mine,' said William.

'It's not fair,' said Kitty. 'Grown-ups never think they have to explain things.'

'They wouldn't like it if we acted the same,' said Rosie.

Just then, the bell went – but Kitty had started to think. And at play-time she told William and Rosie her plan.

'Do you both think we should all be allowed to go to school on our own, instead of being treated like babies?'

'Yes,' said Rosie and William.

'And do you think grown-ups should give proper *reasons*?' Kitty asked.

They agreed.

'Well, here's what we do . . .' said Kitty.

At home that night, Mum asked Kitty when she was going to do her homework.

'Oh, I'm not going to do it,' said Kitty.

'Why ever not?' said Mum, in a surprised voice.

'Because.'

'Because what.'

'Oh, because I say so, that's all,' said Kitty with a grin.

'KITTY!' shouted Mum, and before Kitty had time to explain that they didn't have any homework at all, because their teacher wasn't well, she was sent upstairs to her room, for being cheeky.

Next day the three children compared notes.

'My mum stopped my pocket money,' said William glumly.

'My mum said I couldn't have the fried chicken if I couldn't be polite,' said Rosie, with a big sigh, 'and she wouldn't let me *explain*!'

'Nor would mine,' said William. 'It didn't work, Kit.'

Kitty felt guilty. She had thought that they would give the grown-ups a taste of their own medicine, and then explain and then all the mums would promise not to say 'Because I said so' each time the children asked 'Why not?', and of course they would agree to let them go to school alone . . .

But something had gone wrong.

It simply wasn't fair.

Kitty thought about this all day, and came out of school with a *very* sulky face. In fact, she walked about two metres away from her mother, and wouldn't hold her hand.

'All right, Kitty, what's all this about?' asked Mum.

Kitty explained at last.

'But why didn't you *say* you didn't actually have any homework?' asked Mum, surprised.

'Because *you* never explain,' sniffed Kitty. 'I was just copying you.'

Her mother went very quiet for a few

minutes. Then she stopped suddenly. 'All right, Kitty, I agree with you. So now let's do a little experiment. You walk home on your own. I'm going back to school to have a word with the headmistress, before she leaves. Off you go.'

Kitty was amazed, but she wasn't going to show it. She nodded and marched off down the road, feeling very bold. If she'd looked behind her she would have seen Mum stand behind the bus-shelter and watch her. She didn't go back to school at all. Then after a while, she crept along, some way behind Kitty, keeping her eyes on her all the time.

The road was long, and led past a small park – where sometimes they would go and play on the swings. Kitty wouldn't do that tonight. Not on her own. She could see other children through the railings, playing with their mothers. It looked fun.

On she marched, the road seeming much longer than it usually did. It was strange: Kitty felt so very *small* today. When she got to the zebra crossing the lollipop lady stared at her. 'On your own?' she asked.

'Yes,' said Kitty proudly.

But she felt funny – as if everyone was looking at her.

Once over the road she had to walk down two streets before she came to theirs. Few people were around. A man came towards her, with a small dog on a lead. He smiled at Kitty, but she kept her eyes on the ground. Then she saw a small group of very big boys standing on the street corner, laughing and joking. Kitty was nervous; she didn't want to walk past them.

'Hello, squirt!' one of them called. Kitty's cheeks went very red and she wanted to cry.

Once past them, she started to run. She wanted so much to be home, where it was safe. Suddenly the bushes and trees in the gardens looked as if they were hiding a mysterious

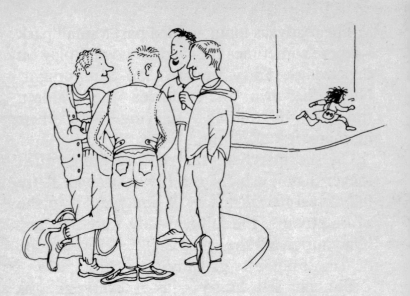

something which might jump out at her.

At last she reached her own gate and rushed inside. She sat down on the front doorstep to wait for Mum – who appeared very soon afterwards.

'Mum,' said Kitty in a small voice, 'I don't want to walk home on my own again.'

'Oh? Why not, dear?' asked Mum.

'Just *because*,' said Kitty.

'Yes . . . and you know, that's just why *I* said no in the first place, darling,' said Mum.

And they didn't have to explain any more.

You Can't Play!

Rosie and Kitty were such good friends that they often spent time together at weekends. Kitty liked Rosie's house, because it was noisy and jolly, but usually Rosie came to Kitty's, because she liked to get away from her family.

'If you had three brothers and a big sister you'd know what I mean,' said Rosie.

'But it's nice to play in a gang,' said Kitty.

'Not when you've got no choice,' said Rosie.

One Saturday morning Rosie's dad dropped her off at Kitty's house, and the two girls munched apples while they decided what to do.

Kitty's brother Daniel came into the kitchen, twirling his cricket bat. 'Anybody want to play french cricket?' he called. Kitty thought it would be fun, and looked across at her friend. But Rosie was frowning and shaking her head, and so Kitty said no.

Daniel shrugged. 'OK – I'll go up the road to Eddie's house. He and Dave will play with me.' And he went out to find his friends.

'What shall we do then, Rosie?' asked Kitty.

'Let's play . . . Snakes and Ladders,' Rosie said.

To be honest, that wasn't what Kitty felt like doing at all – but she liked Rosie so much she agreed. They had a couple of games, then went upstairs to Kitty's room and played with her toy castle and soldiers. Then they decided to clean out Sandy the hamster – which was great fun when there were two of you. They were just finishing, and had already decided to play dressing-up next, when there was a knock on the back door.

It was William, from next door.

'Can I play with you?' he asked.

Before Kitty could open her mouth, Rosie said, 'No.'

William looked surprised. 'Why not?' he asked.

There was a silence. Rosie looked at Kitty and Kitty looked at Rosie, and neither of them knew what to say. Then at last Rosie blurted out, 'Because . . . *you're a boy!*' And, although Kitty felt mean, she laughed.

At that William looked very hurt, and disappeared. Kitty said nothing to Rosie, and they went upstairs to play – but somehow all the fun had gone out of the morning. Soon the doorbell rang and Rosie's dad arrived to collect her.

Kitty saw nothing of William all the rest of the weekend. This was unusual, because he and his sister Sally usually played with Daniel and Kitty at least once. But it was a cold, rainy Sunday, and Kitty thought he was probably happy indoors. She hoped so.

On Monday morning Rosie's place was empty. Kitty asked the teacher where she was, and Mrs Smith said she was ill. At break-time Kitty wandered about, missing Rosie and not knowing what to do.

In a corner of the playground she found William, crouching on the ground with Tom, having races with their tiny, fast pull-back cars.

'Hello Will,' said Kitty, sitting down beside

them. 'Can I watch?'

William turned his back on Kitty. 'No, you can't,' he said coldly.

'Why not?' Kitty asked.

'Because you're a *girl*,' said William, sending his car shooting off so fast it skidded and turned over.

Kitty was furious. She snatched up his car and held it behind her back. 'What's that got to do with it?' she shouted – and then she remembered.

Then Kitty went very red, and felt terrible. Without a word she took her hand from behind her back and held out the car to William. 'I'm sorry,' she said.

He looked at her for what seemed like a long time and then mumbled, 'Oh, all right, you can have a go if you like.'

Soon afterwards they heard the bell. Walking back to the classroom Kitty asked William if he knew the saying, 'Two's company, three's a crowd.'

William said he did.

'Well, that's the only reason Rosie didn't want you to play on Saturday. It wasn't 'cos you're a boy.'

'Oh, it couldn't be,' said William.

'Why not?' asked Kitty in a serious voice.

'Because boys are best!' he joked.

'Not when Rosie's around!' laughed Kitty, so glad they were friends again.

Holiday Plans

One morning Kitty was coming downstairs when she heard Mum and Dad talking. Or rather, she heard their talking drowned by Dan's huge, loud shout, 'OH NO!'

'What's happened?' asked Kitty, rushing into the sitting room.

'Your Aunty Susan and Uncle Joe are going to rent a cottage in Cornwall for the summer holiday,' explained Dad.

'They've asked us to share it with them, and we've said yes,' added Mum.

Now it was Kitty's turn. 'OH NO!' she shouted.

'It's not fair!' Daniel groaned.

'Don't *want* to!' said Kitty.

'But why not?' sighed Mum and Dad together.

'Because we can't stand Melissa!' yelled Kitty. (She had this picture in her mind of her

cousin skipping around the countryside in frilly dresses, never wanting to climb trees or get dirty – she couldn't bear it.)

Kitty was telling the truth, but it made Mum angry. 'Right,' she said firmly. 'If you're going to be mean about your cousin I don't want to talk to you. We're going to Cornwall, and that's that.'

Dad sat down to read the newspaper, Mum went into the kitchen and Daniel beckoned to Kitty. She followed him into the hall.

'We didn't handle that very well, Kit,' he

whispered, looking thoughtful. 'Now listen – I think we should start again . . .'

A little while later (giving Mum the time to calm down), Daniel and Kitty called both their parents into the sitting room. 'We're going to have a family meeting,' said Kitty.

Daniel took charge. He stood in front of the fireplace and Kitty sat on the arm of the chair near him. Mum and Dad sat on the sofa, wondering what was going to happen.

'Right,' said Daniel, 'remember we all said we wanted to go on a barge holiday this summer? 'Cos Dad loves the water?'

'Er . . . yes,' said Mum.

'Remember you *promised*?' muttered Kitty – but Dan gave her a warning look and she said no more.

'We all talked about it together, didn't we?' asked Dan.

Mum and Dad nodded.

'Right. Well, we say we don't want to go to Cornwall, and you ask why not. Shall I tell you why?'

Kitty bit her lips together, to stop herself from saying the wrong thing. Dad was looking amused. 'Yes, go on, Dan, you're like someone on television!' He smiled.

'Because you didn't ask *us*, that's why. You didn't talk to us.'

'Families should do things together,' blurted Kitty.

'Including making decisions,' said Daniel.

'Right?' said Kitty, putting her hands on her hips.

'Right!' said Daniel, folding his arms. 'So I've worked out the answer to the whole problem.'

'What's that?' asked Mum.

'We hire a big boat and invite Aunty Susan, Uncle Joe and Melissa to share it with *us*,' said Daniel.

Kitty nearly fell off the chair. She looked at her brother, opened her mouth like a fish –

then closed it again, when Daniel gave her a warning look.

'We did *promise* them we'd go on a boat,' said Dad.

'And I suppose that *would* be a way out,' said Mum. 'Anyway, they'll be here in a minute, so we can ask them.'

When the doorbell rang Kitty hissed, 'Dan, what are you doing? I can't stand Meliss . . .'

'Shut up, Kit,' he whispered, giving her a sharp kick.

When Aunty Susan and Uncle Joe were sitting with coffee and biscuits, and Melissa had finished smiling snootily at Kitty's dirty dungarees, Dan said, 'Aren't you going to ask them, Mum?'

Their mother explained how they'd forgotten their promise to take the children on a river or canal holiday and how Daniel had come up with this wonderful plan of sharing a boat, instead of a cottage. 'They *so* want to be with Melissa,' she added.

Everybody looked at Melissa, who shuddered. 'Ugh,' she said, 'I don't want to go on a nasty, cold, wet boat. I can't swim. And anyway, I want to be in a pretty cottage, with roses round the door.'

And that was that.

When the visitors had gone, Kitty looked at

Daniel with admiration. 'You're the cleverest boy in the world, Dan,' she said.

'No,' he said airily, 'I just know our lovely cousin!'

Mr Tubs Goes for a Swim

The school term seemed to whizz by, and soon Kitty and Daniel were packing excitedly.

'You can't take many things on a barge,' warned Mum. But Kitty came downstairs dragging two enormous bags of toys. There was her castle, the soldiers, the garage, three boxes of paints (different colours had run out in each one), two drawing books, crayons, a pile of books, her toy dog, a sticker album, three board games, five card games and a toy picnic set. Oh, and (of course) Mr Tubs, her favourite bear.

'Is all that necessary, Kit?' asked Dad.

Kitty nodded.

'Sorry, love, you'll have to make choices,' said Mum firmly, 'and only take what you really need. After all, we're only away for ten days.'

So it was that Kitty arrived on the barge

27

carrying a drawing book, crayons, two card games, some books, and Mr Tubs – because she couldn't ever sleep without him.

They loved the barge because it was just like a little house inside. Kitty raced around exploring – opening cupboards, choosing her bed, and admiring the neat little stove in the galley-kitchen. She decided right away that she must copy the pretty painted designs on the outside.

Soon it was time to set off, but first Dad

said, 'Now listen, gang, we're on a canal, and so there have to be certain rules . . .' Kitty heard his voice in the distance – but she wasn't listening. She was thinking what fun it would be to live on a barge like this always.

For two days, or maybe three, everything was perfect. The weather was wonderful, the days seemed exciting – and Kitty was very good.

Then came a chilly, rainy day, and Mum told Kitty not to go up on deck. 'Why not?' she protested, grabbing her mac and starting for the steps.

'Because it's pouring down.'

'Daniel's outside.'

'Dan's helping Dad,' said Mum.

'He's always got something to do,' said Kitty, sulkily.

Soon the sun shone again, and Kitty picked up Mr Tubs and wandered out on to the deck. She made her way up to the front of the barge. The light danced on the water, and gleamed on the damp trees – but Kitty didn't notice. She still felt cross.

'I wish you were the captain, Mr Tubs,' she whispered into her bear's furry neck. 'Then nobody would be allowed to give *me* orders.'

She placed Mr Tubs on top of the cabin roof, so that he could *look* as if he were in

29

charge. Just then Dad, who was standing some way away at the back of the barge, glanced up and saw her.

'Hey, don't do that, Kit,' he called. Kitty pretended not to hear. They were always telling her what to do!

'KITTY!' Dad shouted, so that it was impossible for her not to hear. 'I said don't put anything on the roof!'

Kitty glared at him and tossed her head. 'WHY NOT?' she yelled, then folded her arms, and sat down – staring hard at the canal tow-path.

It was a pity she didn't look at the water instead. For just at that moment another barge passed them, going the opposite way. It was bigger and it was faster, and the people on it waved cheerfully.

As it moved through the water it set up large waves behind it, making them rock violently from side to side. Dimly Kitty remembered Dad saying something about that on their first day, and about not leaving anything on the roof . . .

Quickly she jumped up – in time to see Mr Tubs rock, then topple over and slowly roll down the side of the roof and into the water.

Horror! Kitty screamed and started to cry.

For a few seconds she did not dare to open her eyes. She felt helpless. But then she heard shouts – and laughter. At last she forced herself to look.

Dad was standing smiling at her – and holding a dripping teddy bear high in the air. Luckily he had seen what had happened, had quickly leaned over the low side of the barge and grabbed Mr Tubs before he sank.

'Isn't it about time you taught your bear to swim?' smiled Dad.

'Two more seconds, Kit, and his fur would have been water-logged,' said Daniel, in his 'you've-learned-a-lesson' voice.

For once Kitty didn't mind. She took Mr Tubs and helped Dad shake and pummel some of the water out of him, then laid him gently on a towel, in a safe and sheltered part of the boat, to dry in the sun.

Then she went to Dad and put her hand in his. 'Dad,' she said, 'can I make you a promise?'

'Of course, Kitty-kat, what is it?'

'I promise you I'll never ask *why not* again!'

Dad put his arm round her, gave her a huge hug and whispered, 'Now don't you think you should be careful – of making promises you can't possibly keep?'

Trick or Treat?

In the days before Hallowe'en all the shops were full of witch hats, rubber spiders, plastic skeletons, masks, and lots of other spooky toys and decorations. Kitty loved them. Something thrilling was in the air – and she wanted to take part.

Their classroom was decorated with cut-out witches and broomsticks, and Mrs Smith told them lots of legends and customs about Hallowe'en.

'Are you going out trick-or-treating tomorrow night?' asked Rosie, when break-time came.

Kitty said she wasn't sure.

'I am. There's three of us in our road and we always go out together. We dress up, knock on lots of doors and get sweets and biscuits. You can come if you like.'

Kitty jumped up and down with excitement.

'Oh, thank you, Rosie, I'd love to. It'll be the best Hallowe'en ever.'

That night she was collected by William and his mum, and as soon as she reached home Kitty rushed into the sitting room and told her mother about the plan.

'Oh,' said Mum – in that voice Kitty knew well. It meant, 'You-aren't-going-to-like-what-I'm-going-to-say.'

'Well? Won't it be fun?' demanded Kitty.

'Darling, you can't go trick-or-treating,' said Mum.

'WHY NOT?'

'Because . . .' Kitty looked at her, and

35

waited. 'Yes, I know I've got to explain. Well, if you go and knock on people's doors . . . er . . . you might frighten old ladies.'

'Mum! That's a *silly* reason. Rosie said . . .'

'I don't care what Rosie said; *I* say you can't go.'

'But *why not*?' wailed Kitty again – looking really unhappy, as well as angry.

Mum was quiet for a few minutes. Then she took hold of Kitty's arm, and pulled her on to her lap.

'Come on, let's have a little talk. Shall I tell you the truth?'

Kitty nodded.

Mum took a deep breath. 'This isn't easy, Kitty – the truth is, I don't want you wandering the streets in the dark.'

'But I'd be with the others,' protested Kitty.

'Yes, but you might get separated from them. Children can be silly when they're excited. And you know, darling, real people can be much worse than imaginary witches, you know. You don't know *who* is wandering about the town at night – and so I won't let you go out. It's because I love you. Don't you see?'

'Couldn't the three of *us* go out, you, me, and Daniel?' pleaded Kitty.

Mum shook her head. Kitty jumped up and sighed. 'Well, I'll have to tell the others that

my Hallowe'en will be the most *boring* ever! Thanks a lot, Mum!' And she ran out of the room, leaving her mother sitting in the chair, looking a bit sad and thoughtful.

Next day she told Rosie what had happened. Her friend shrugged. 'Well, I suppose my mum wouldn't let me go if my big sister didn't come with us. Didn't you explain?'

'Oh, Mum wouldn't have listened. You know what grown-ups are like, once they've made up their minds . . .'

Rosie nodded. She understood.

On the way home from school Kitty was unusually quiet. So was Mum. When they got to the house Mum said, 'Why don't you go upstairs and play in your room?'

'All right,' said Kitty, in a cool voice.

Soon she heard Dan come in, talk to Mum, then come upstairs. He suggested he and Kitty play a game in her room – which surprised her, because usually he wanted to watch television. 'I'll just go downstairs and get some biscuits,' she said, pleased.

'No!' cried Dan, then added, 'Er, I'm not hungry. Let's get on with the game.' Kitty thought that was strange.

After about forty minutes Daniel looked at his watch and said, 'Now – let's go downstairs.' Without thinking Kitty followed him. The hall lights were off, but a candle flickered on the table at the bottom of the stairs. Now that was *very* strange.

'Don't be scared, Kit,' whispered Dan, with an odd smile.

They pushed open the kitchen door . . . and

Kitty got a shock. The room was dark, lit only by a few candles. A huge orange pumpkin head grinned and glowed in the middle of the table – which was covered with a black cloth. On a chair sat . . . a ghost: a small, white lumpy shape, with round black eyes.

As Kitty moved forward nervously, something fine and tickly brushed across her face, so that she jumped back with a yelp. *Cobwebs*.

And there, by the stove, stirring a huge pot, was a tall figure, wearing a pointed hat and a black cloak. It turned and Kitty saw that her face was all white, marked with heavy black lines and spots, and surrounded by thick grey hair. 'Welcome to the witch's kitchen, little girl,' she cackled.

Now, in her *mind* Kitty knew it was Mum. But in her *heart* she believed this was a real witch and she felt rather nervous! The witch dipped her spoon into the pot and pulled out a horrible wriggling snake. Then she made Kitty touch the enormous black furry spider that sat on the table, and as she reached out it jumped – making Kitty jump too.

'Now, little girl, if you want to escape from my kitchen, you and your brother must duck for apples. If you don't bite an apple, you're my prisoner forever!' And she shrieked with cackling laughter again.

Kitty's mind thought, 'Mum's a good actress.' But her heart thought, 'Help!'

The witch brought out a large bowl of water, on which some apples bobbed – and Kitty and

Daniel got wet faces and hair trying to grab them with their mouths. It was such fun.

Then the witch gave them dried insects to eat (which looked very like crisps) and blood to drink (which tasted just like blackcurrant juice).

Suddenly the light snapped on and there was Dad.

'What's going on?' he began, staring at his dripping children. Then he looked at Mum, and laughed.

They showed him the jumpy plastic spider and the rubber snake, then pulled the sheet off the funny, lumpy little ghost – who turned out to be Mr Tubs. The 'cobwebs' were long pieces of black cotton, pinned up on the door frame.

'It was a trick *and* a treat, Dad,' said Kitty.

At last Mum pulled off her hat, with the long woollen hair attached – she still looked funny, with her ugly make-up – and Kitty ran and threw her arms around her.

'I don't want you to stop being a witch,' she whispered.

'Why not?' smiled Mum.

'Because now I know that witches are the nicest, kindest people in the world,' said Kitty.

The Visit

Gran was in hospital. Mum and Dad looked worried most of the time and went to see her often. Kitty painted her a beautiful get-well card and took it to show Mum.

'I'll take it to her this afternoon – when you go,' Kitty said.

'It's really beautiful, love, and it'll make her feel better – but you can't come and visit,' said Mum.

'Why not?' asked Kitty – of course.

'Because . . . because Gran's *very* ill this time,' said Mum, looking serious. Then Kitty felt very sad.

'But she will get better, won't she, Mum? You've got to tell me the truth – because I'm older now.'

Mum didn't speak at first. She seemed to be thinking hard. Then she sat down at the kitchen table, and sighed. 'No, Kitty, I don't think she will get better.'

'But *why not*?' wailed Kitty.

'Because she's got something the matter with her which the doctors aren't sure how to cure. And Gran is very old, you see, so it makes it harder . . .'

'Oh,' said Kitty. She didn't know what else to say.

In her own room, she thought and thought. She looked at all her toys, her bed with its patterned duvet, all the cuddly animals on their shelf and the posters on the walls – all the things she most liked. And she decided that she'd happily give them all away if only Gran could get better.

After a while Dad came in to talk to her, and she told him how she felt.

'Dad – I don't want you and Mum to get old.'

He smiled. 'I was going to ask "why not?", like you always do, but I know why not. We never want people we love to change. The thing is, Kit, *everybody* has to grow old.'

Kitty shivered. 'But it's so sad! Oh, why can't we always stay the same forever, you and Mum, me and Dan – and Gran?'

Dad put out his arm and hugged her. He was smiling very gently. 'Because we can't, Kit – and that's a fact. Look, even Sandy the hamster is getting older. And the trees . . . everything! Even your old dad. And *that's* why we mustn't waste precious time being miserable. Now, how do you fancy a choc ice?'

A few days went by, and Mum and Dad looked more worried than ever. They went to the hospital a lot, and the phone rang, and Aunty Susan came round . . . and Kitty knew that Gran had had a big operation. It was scary.

She and Dan talked and wished they knew what was going on. But they had to go to school and get on with things – Mum said.

But, *'What if Gran dies?'* whispered Kitty.

Then one afternoon William's mum brought her home from school and she ran into the house – to find Mum with her coat on, looking like someone with a secret. Dad came in with Daniel and asked, 'Are we all ready?'

'Where are we going?' asked Kitty.

'It's a surprise,' said Mum.

Kitty recognised the way they were going. It led to the hospital. She felt very nervous and wanted to ask questions, but didn't dare.

They walked along corridors which smelt funny, past nurses and doctors, and Kitty felt even more afraid. But Mum and Dad held her hands and Daniel looked so cheerful . . .

At last they reached the ward – there, sitting up in bed, looking a bit pale, but lovely with

her hair in a bun, was Gran. She wore a frilly bed-jacket.

Flowers and cards surrounded her, with Kitty's card right in the middle. Gran was smiling widely and held out her arms to Kitty – who would have jumped on the bed, only it was too high.

'Be gentle, Kitty,' said Mum, 'Gran's had a bad time.'

'Oh, but I'm better now,' said Gran, holding Dan's hand one side of the bed and Kitty's the other. 'I'm much tougher than everybody thinks, you know!'

Then she gave Daniel and Kitty big bars of chocolate she had bought from the hospital trolley. Mum took out packets of biscuits and drinks for the children, and a nurse brought the grown-ups some tea.

'This is Gran's get-well party, isn't it?' said Kitty happily.

'Oh no,' said Gran, 'I wouldn't want a get-well party.'

'Why not?' asked Kitty.

'Because I AM well!' laughed Gran.

Kitty's Great Idea

Kitty was watching television one evening when she had a great idea. The programme was about nature and how it was really important to leave old hedges alone so that wild flowers could grow, and small animals and insects make their homes.

Now Kitty's parents believed in letting nature have its own way. They didn't use any artificial things to make the grass grow, or kill weeds. 'Weeds can be so pretty,' said Kitty's mum. 'In the country they're called wild flowers!'

So their garden was wild and the hedge that ran along the bottom was huge and tangly. It was easy to imagine whole families of mice having a little city there, just like in the picture books. They were all proud of that hedge.

But the man who lived behind their house (so that the hedge was between their gardens), kept complaining about it. His garden was really neat. He said the hedge was too high and too messy and Kitty's dad got very angry because Mr Simpson tried to make it thinner.

'Oh, dear, it's terrible quarrelling with neighbours,' said Kitty's mum. 'If only people could see that nature *matters*.'

So Kitty had her great idea.

'Mum,' she said, 'why don't we open our garden so people can come and see it? Like in those posh houses? We can have a collection, for a nature charity or something. And we could invite that man we saw on TV – the one in the government who's in charge of the in . . . in . . .'

'Environment,' said Daniel, with a grin.

'Don't be so stupid, Kitty, that would *never* work!'

'Why not?' said Kitty.

'Because, darling, it's a sweet, but impossible idea,' smiled Mum.

Kitty folded her arms. This was a challenge. 'All right then, what's the name of that man?'

'Mr Thornton – Christopher Thornton,' said Mum. 'But really, Kitty . . .'

Kitty didn't wait to hear the rest. She went up into her bedroom and got out the new box of rainbow-coloured stationery she had been given for her birthday. Then, very, very carefully, in her best handwriting, she wrote two letters – setting them out just as they had been shown in school.

First she wrote to the local paper and told them that her family had a wild garden with a beautiful hedge and lots of butterflies – and because everybody had to be interested in the environment (she had to look that up in her dictionary) she would be opening the garden to the public on Saturday 20 April.

Then she wrote to Christopher Thornton, telling him the same thing and asking him to come along and see. She didn't quite know where to send this letter, so this was how she addressed it:

Mr Christopher Thornton, MP.
The Man in Charge of the Environment,
The Government,
House of Parliament, LONDON.

She went and asked for two stamps, and frowned because Mum and Dad were still laughing at her.

'They'll never write back to you,' said Daniel.

'Why not?'

'Because you're only a little girl,' he replied.

'You'll see,' she muttered.

A week passed, and nothing happened. Every morning Kitty looked for letters, but none came. 20 April was five days away. She felt very disappointed.

Then, on Monday morning, Dad came into breakfast waving an envelope. It was typed and addressed to Kitty. They all watched as she opened it. This is what it said:

Dear Kitty,
   Thank you for your lovely letter.
It is very nice to know that children like
you are so interested in nature. I like
wild gardens too.
   As it happens I have to make a speech in
a town very near yours on Saturday night.
So I could come along on the way and see
your lovely garden and wonderful old hedge.
We should be there at about three o'clock
and look forward to meeting you
and your parents.

Your sincerely,
Christopher Thornton
(The Man in Charge of the Environment)

Kitty thought Mum would faint. Dad sat down heavily and gasped, 'Well, who would have thought . . .?' And Kitty just stuck out her tongue at Daniel and said, '*See!*'

That night the telephone rang and the local paper asked if they could come and take a photograph of Kitty by the hedge. When Dad

told them that Christopher Thornton was coming to visit they got very excited and said they'd write about that too. On the Friday there was a picture of Kitty – with a short article saying she was opening their garden in aid of a charity which tried to save the environment – and that she had actually got Mr Thornton to come.

Saturday 20 April was a beautiful clear day. Kitty and Daniel set up a table by the gate, and waited. Sure enough, people started to arrive, each one putting 15p into a box. They'd all seen the newspaper. By the time it came to the afternoon there was quite a crowd.

Just before three o'clock lots of

photographers arrived, and when the sleek black car pulled up at their gate there was such a noise of clicking and such a buzz of excitement Kitty felt quite afraid. But Christopher Thornton beamed at her and shook her hand in front of all the cameras. When Kitty told him he had to put his money in the box everybody roared with laughter – she didn't know why.

It was like a dream. Kitty showed Mr Thornton, and the people with him, all around the garden and they spent a long time admiring the hedge and talking with Dad about things called pesticides and weed-killers which did harm.

Then Mum gave them tea (using her best china, of course) and it was time to go. But before he left, Christopher Thornton hugged

Kitty, saying she reminded him of his own little girl and he gave her a lovely book about wild-life.

As they went down the front path to say goodbye, Kitty noticed bad-tempered Mr Simpson, from the house behind, standing by the front gate and staring so hard she thought his eyes would fall out of his head.

Dad didn't miss the chance. With a twinkle

in his eye he introduced Mr Thornton, saying, 'This is another of our neighbours. The hedge borders his garden too.'

'Does it? Well, I think you're very lucky,' smiled Christopher Thornton, shaking Mr Simpson's hand.

'Er . . . thank you . . . er . . . oh yes, I know. Nice to meet you,' stuttered their neighbour – pink with pleasure at meeting someone so important.

And then Kitty knew that her great idea – the one they'd called impossible – had worked, even beyond her wildest dreams. For they wouldn't have any trouble with Mr Simpson again!

The Puzzle

Kitty was bored. She couldn't go to William's house because he had 'flu, and when she rang Rosie to see if she could come over to play, there was no reply. And it was pouring with rain.

'Will you play a game with me, Daniel?' Kitty asked, wandering into his room.

'No, Kit,' he said, hunched over his desk.

'Why not?'

'Because I want to finish this model aeroplane and it's really fiddly,' he said, without even looking up.

So Kitty went downstairs to find Dad. He wasn't in the sitting room, but Kitty heard the clatter of plates and found him in the kitchen, washing the breakfast things.

'Dad – shall we have a game of Monopoly? You know it's your favourite and you always win . . .' asked Kitty, in a wheedling voice.

'Sorry, Kit,' said Dad, wiping his hands.

'Why not?' she asked, feeling disappointed, because Dad was usually such fun.

'Because I've got to finish this and it's my turn to cook lunch today, so I'm going to do that next – it's a dish that needs a long time in the oven.'

'Boring!' said Kitty.

'You'd say that if there was no lunch,' grinned Dad.

Then Kitty went in search of Mum and found her at the desk in the sitting room.

'Mum,' said Kitty, 'will you *do* something with me?'

'I'm sorry, my love . . .' said Mum in that voice Kitty hated – all far away, as if she hadn't really heard at all.

'Why *not*?' said Kitty. She felt very sulky now.

'Because I've got to do this work, ready for my job on Monday,' said Mum, her fingers tapping the calculator as she spoke. 'Honestly, Kit, surely you're old enough to be able to play on your own.'

Kitty went upstairs and sat down at her own desk. It was so boring, she thought, that people always said 'No' to things, instead of trying to work out how they could happen . . .

Something made her take a piece of plain paper and write 'WHY NOT' and then 'SEE HOW'. She looked at those four words for quite a while, drawing boxes around them and wondering what to do. 'How to change the "why not" into the "see how" . . .' she murmured, staring at the words and starting to think.

She had found something to do. It took quite a while, but Kitty had great fun working it out. At last she took three clean sheets of paper, wrote out her puzzle on each one and ran downstairs.

First she went into the sitting room. She knew Mum could never resist a challenge. 'Here you are, Mum,' she said. 'I've worked out a puzzle for you. Bet you can't do it!'

'Oh, you do, do you? Let's see,' said Mum.

This was on the paper:

WHY NOT

. . . . . .

. . . . . .

. . . . . .

. . . . . .

SEE HOW

'You've got to change "why not" into "see how", changing only one letter each time, on each whole line,' Kitty explained. 'But one letter stays the same all the way.'

'This should be easy,' said Mum.

Just then Dad came into the room. 'What's going on?' he asked. Kitty explained. Mum was too busy staring at the puzzle and doodling with her pencil on a spare bit of paper to say anything.

'Bet you can't beat Mum,' smiled Kitty.

'Oh yes?' said Dad. He put down his wooden spoon on Mum's papers, grabbed a pencil and sat down in a chair.

Kitty ran upstairs and told Daniel there was a competition. He put down his glue like a shot and ran downstairs.

'Should be easy,' he said, 'once you know the "o" stays the same.'

'Well, *try*,' said Kitty.

'Sshh,' said Mum and Dad together.

Some time later, Mum laughed, and said she'd got it. Dad put down his pencil and groaned. Daniel asked Kitty for the answer. (But see if you can do it, before you look.)

'Easy,' she said. 'This is how it goes . . .'

WHY NOT
WHY NOW
SHY NOW
SHE NOW
SEE NOW
SEE HOW

Mum and Dad smiled and Dad said, 'Is there a message in this, Kit-Kat?'

Kitty nodded. 'Yes, instead of thinking of reasons *not* to do things, why not try to see how we *can* do things?'

'Ahah!' said Dad.

'Well, I won,' said Mum, 'so what's my prize?'

'A family game of Monopoly,' said Kitty. 'And before you all say "No", I've worked out how. You all do what you're doing for twenty more minutes and *then* we play.'

'That, Kitty,' said Dad, 'is what grown-ups call a compromise.'

'And it proves our girl is growing up,' said Mum, ruffling Kitty's hair.

'No I'm not,' said Kitty.

'Why not?' asked Mum.

'Because when you're grown-up you don't want to play games,' said Kitty.

'Oh yes, we do,' roared Dad, 'in fact – we'll play NOW!'